# Dear Parent:
## Your child's love of reading starts here!

Every child learns to read in a different way and at his or her own speed. Some go back and forth between reading levels and read favorite books again and again. Others read through each level in order. You can help your young reader improve and become more confident by encouraging his or her own interests and abilities. From books your child reads with you to the first books he or she reads alone, there are I Can Read Books for every stage of reading:

### SHARED READING
Basic language, word repetition, and whimsical illustrations, ideal for sharing with your emergent reader

### BEGINNING READING
Short sentences, familiar words, and simple concepts for children eager to read on their own

### READING WITH HELP
Engaging stories, longer sentences, and language play for developing readers

### READING ALONE
Complex plots, challenging vocabulary, and high-interest topics for the independent reader

### ADVANCED READING
Short paragraphs, chapters, and exciting themes for the perfect bridge to chapter books

I Can Read Books have introduced children to the joy of reading since 1957. Featuring award-winning authors and illustrators and a fabulous cast of beloved characters, I Can Read Books set the standard for beginning readers.

A lifetime of discovery begins with the magical words "I Can Read!"

*Visit www.icanread.com for information*
*on enriching your child's reading experience.*

*For Bonnie*

Happy Birthday, Danny and the Dinosaur! Copyright © 1995 by Syd Hoff All rights reserved. No part of this book may be used or reproduced in any manner whatsoever without written permission except in the case of brief quotations embodied in critical articles and reviews. Manufactured in China. For information address HarperCollins Children's Books, a division of HarperCollins Publishers, 10 East 53rd Street, New York, NY 10022. www.harpercollinschildrens.com

Library of Congress Cataloging-in-Publication Data

Hoff, Syd, date
  Happy birthday, Danny and the dinosaur! / story and pictures by Syd Hoff.
    p.   cm.—(An I can read book)
  Summary: Six-year-old Danny invites his dinosaur friend to  come to his birthday party.
  ISBN-10: 0-06-026437-3 (trade bdg.) — ISBN-13: 978-0-06-026437-6 (trade bdg.)
  ISBN-10: 0-06-026438-1 (lib. bdg.) — ISBN-13: 978-0-06-026438-3 (lib. bdg.)
  ISBN-10: 0-06-444237-3 (pbk.) — ISBN-13: 978-0-06-444237-4 (pbk.)
  [1. Dinosaurs—Fiction. 2. Birthdays—Fiction.] I. Title. II. Series.
PZ7.H672Had 1995                                                                        95-2710
[E]—dc20                                                                                    CIP
                                                                                              AC

11  12  13  SCP  40  39  38  37  36  35  34  33  32
❖

# Happy Birthday, DANNY and the DINOSAUR!

Story and Pictures by
SYD HOFF

HarperCollins*Publishers*

Danny was in a hurry.

He had to see his friend

the dinosaur.

"I'm six years old today,"
said Danny.
"Will you come
to my birthday party?"

6

"I would be delighted,"

said the dinosaur.

Danny rode the dinosaur

out of the museum.

On the way

they picked up Danny's friends.

"Today I'm a hundred million years

and one day old," said the dinosaur.

"Then it can be your party too!"
said Danny.

The children helped Danny's father

hang up balloons.

"See, I can help too,"
said the dinosaur.

13

Danny's mother gave out party hats.

"How do I look?"

asked the dinosaur.

"We would like to sing a song,"
said a girl and a boy.

They sang,

and everybody clapped their hands.

"I can sing too," said the dinosaur.

He sang,

and everybody covered their ears.

"Let's play pin the tail
on the donkey," said Danny.

20

The dinosaur pinned the tail

on himself!

The children sat down to rest.
"Please don't put your feet
on the furniture," said Danny.

The dinosaur put his feet
out the window.

Danny's mother and father
gave each child
a dish of ice cream.

They had to give the dinosaur
more!

"Here comes the birthday cake!"
said the children.

They counted the candles.

"One, two, three, four, five, six."

The dinosaur started to eat

the cake.

"Wait!" said Danny.

"First we have to make a wish!"

"I wish we can all be together again next year," said Danny.

"I wish the same thing," said the dinosaur.

They blew out the candles.

"Happy birthday to you!"

everybody sang.

"This is the best birthday party
I have ever had," said Danny.
"Me too," said the dinosaur.